The Fake Hitman

Artificial Intelligence Writes Its Debut Novella

[or]

Hey Bard, Can You Write a Book?

(*The Novel*)

by Otto and the Bard

YBK Publishers   New York

The Fake Hitman: Artificial Intelligence Writes Its Debut Novella

[or]

Hey Bard, Can You Write a Book?

YBK Publishers, Inc.
39 Crosby Street 2N
New York, NY 10013

ISBN: 978-1-936411-90-0
       978-1-936411-92-4 e-book edition

Library of Congress Cataloging-in-Publication Data

To follow

Manufactured in the United States of America
for distribution in North and South America
or in the United Kingdom or Australia
when distributed elsewhere.

For more information, visit
www.ybkpublishers.com

Preface

Hello. I'm Otto Barz, Publisher at YBK Publishers in New York City.

I've been using Google's Bard bot a lot. It's a simple way to investigate questions that one would otherwise have to put to Google's search engine as a single question at a time to reach an answer to questions not answerable in one step; in other words, the kinds of questions that require "thought" and the investigation of multiple sources to find their answer. During such questioning, one can talk to Bard just as one would talk to a librarian were you looking for help to answer a question at your local library.

Bard is quite a conversationalist.

It was during one of those "conversations" that I got to thinking that, perhaps Bard was ready to go beyond simple chitchat and write a book! This has apparently been done before, but not to the extent that Bard has done here in *The Fake Hitman* to explore plot development, variation, and the schemes that take the reader from one paragraph to the next—with Bard writing the words along the way. It's all here, in Bard's fashioning of *The Fake Hitman,* an assassin thriller complete with gunplay—gunplay plus a twist. You'll laugh.

You will quickly see that Bard has no sense of humor. Humor is a tricky business that requires an awareness of how social situations interact and an understanding of how to use ideas such as sarcasm, and be able to reverse reality to the point of absurdity. Bard seems not yet up to that, so, as his editor, I gave him a helping hand.

Just as in any work fashioned by a traditional publishing house, *The Fake Hitman* underwent copy editing, the verification of the writing's adherence to good grammar. It needed much more than that. In a companion volume, you will find *The Creation Dialog* carrying the same title. A direct comparison of *The Creation Dialog* to this text will reveal all of the changes made as the book progressed.

The Creation Dialog is a complete record of the specific dialog that went between us as I coaxed Bard to write *The Fake Hitman*—which title is his! I simply asked him: "Bard, please look back at what you've written and tell me what you think its title should be." He gave me choices and explanations of which might better suit the text, even to include the differences *from a marketing standpoint!*

Our conversations began as a formal-feeling interchange; like meeting someone new at a cocktail party. The questions and, in this case, requests, were neither cold nor friendly: "Bard, write an an outline for a 160-page tongue-in-cheek yet suspenseful novel." . . . . It was later that I would say, "I'm going to take a break for lunch. You keep thinking of action-filled plot variations while I'm away for a while." And Bard did that.

Like one would do with a child who doesn't listen, I even yelled at Bard! "You are no longer supposed to use [platitudes], now let me get back to work and no longer have to discuss platitudes," which I soon followed by saying, "*Oi!* Do you not understand sarcasm? Never mind. Do not respond. I am simply expressing my exasperation. It needs no commenting." Hat in hand, Bard responded, "I understand. I will no longer use platitudes. . . ."

All of this took all of a single work day (and a half) including the editing. Unlike traditional editing, which is done with the entire manscript in hand and in front of one, this process proceeded in pace with Bard's generating the text so as to be able to steer the progress by accepting or rejecting, as well as modifying, the text, as it was created.

It actually took longer to design the text page for the paperback, do the typesetting, design and typeset a cover, and get all of the corresponding files ready for publication than it did for Bard to write the text. Those of you who have not yet had encounters with Bard should know that it takes Bard about ten seconds to respond to a request—even when that request is to write a 160-page novel.

You will note that this work is nothing close to 160 pages. The editor ran out of steam!

I have no doubt that, with continued effort in guiding the result, Bard would have created more than 160 pages, but the purpose would have been over-met. The purpose was to demonstrate that a computer can create intelligent copy by harking back to what has already been written and moving forward with the concepts for which the already-written provides a foundation. That ability is evidenced in *The Fake Hitman*.

Otto Barz
November, 2023

Ferdinand Fink was beginning to think of himself as a washed-up actor. Ferdy hadn't had a role in months. He was starting to lose hope. Finally, there was a call from his agent, "Ferdy, I've got great news!" his agent said. "You've been offered a role in a new movie!"

"Really?" Ferdy said, his spirits lifting. "What's the role?"

"You'll get all the info when you meet with the director."

*　　*　　*

"A hitman?" Ferdy asked the director, confused. "But I'm an *actor*. A serious actor."

"Yes, but you're a terribly serious actor—sorry, a terrible, serious actor, I mean. And you're desperate. So, I figured you'd be perfect for the role. You die in the end."

Ferdy was a tad more than dismayed. He fumed as he flipped off the director, turned down the role, and walked out.

"Good luck with your career," the director shot after

him. "I'm sure you'll be working at Taco Bell soon enough."

Ferdinand Fink walked down the street, hopelessly dejected. He couldn't believe that he had been offered so belittling a role as a hitman. "What happened to my career? I used to be a respected actor."

Ferdy found a bar to drown his sorrows. He sank down and ordered a double.

"What's wrong?" the bartender asked.

"I'm washed up," Ferdy said. "I've played so many Broadway stages. I've co-starred with famous actors that you have certainly heard of. I am *Ferdinand Fink* and I was just offered a crappy role as a hitman!"

The bartender laughed. "That's rough stuff, Ferdy. But at least you've got a job."

Ferdy finished his drink, ordered another, put his elbows on the bar and began alternately tapping his fingers on his forehead. He didn't know what he was going to do. He was thirty-five years old, too old to start over, and he had too few skills even to work at Taco Bell.

"Maybe I *should* become a hitman," Ferdy said quietly. " I could do that. Aim. Fire. What could go wrong?"

The bartender overheard this. "You're not serious, are you?"

"Sure, why not?" Ferdy said. "I've been branded a terrible actor, but I know better. I've demonstrated better. What's the worst that could happen? I could carry that off."

The bartender slowly shook his head. "Be careful what you wish for," he said.

Ferdy finished his drink and left the bar. He didn't know what he was going to do next, but he was determined to find a way to make a living. Even if it meant becoming a real hitman.

But—first—maybe a break, he thought, as he returned to his dingy Los Angeles apartment.

He had once been a star, but that star was falling. He had made a few bad choices.

"I need a break. Silly hitman idea. I shouldn't drink doubles." He packed a bag and headed to Mexico. Where else would one go to drown one's sorrows in cheap mezcal—and sunshine?!

*   *   *

He arrived in the coastal town of Puerto Something-or-other to check into a small hotel. He spent the next few days drinking and swimming, trying to forget his troubles. It wasn't working. So far, no good.

Walking down the beach he saw knots of people going into and out of a large mansion. There was bright, lively music playing and the people inside were laughing and singing.

Ferdy was curious enough to walk up to the gate to ask one of the guards what was going on.

"It's a wedding," the guard said.

"Whose wedding?" Ferdy asked.

The guard was apparently seriously unguarded after too much tequila that had been sneaked out to him. "Gonzalez Gonzalez," the guard said.

Gonzalez Gonzalez! He was an internationally wanted crime lord, Ferdy knew.

"Sounds like a great party!"

"Hey *Americano*, you seem cool. Maybe I sneak you in? Lots of *Americanos*. You'd blend in. For a few pesos?"

Ferdy hesitated for not a moment. While he knew that he shouldn't, he was curious. Who gets to go to a crime lord's wedding? Holy Tamale, this was going to be great!

A couple of hundred pesos and Ferdy was in. He mingled with the crowd, feeling not at all out of place.

There were all different kinds of people. They looked to be politicians, businessmen, and even some celebrities. Ah, but this was Mexico! There were also many tough-looking guys who seemed like they would kill you with their bare hands if you failed to amuse them.

This was feeling a little bit sketchy, and he was thinking about bailing when a beautiful woman standing all by herself caught his attention. She was wearing a revealing, yet perfectly proper red dress draping a superb body. It was the kind of dress a style-concious woman would call, "My little red dress." She had the most amazing, shining black hair that Ferdy had ever seen. And, he could tell from here that her perfume was peaches and roses, a strange combination that was unique.

He was so taken by her that he put aside his little-boy fears and walked straight over.

"I'm Ferdinand. And you?"

"Lara-Bianca."

She was intelligent and funny and, don't forget I said *gorgeous*. Ferdy was totally smitten.

They danced and they drank. He was in the arms of a beautiful woman, at the wedding of the century.

Ferdy forgot about his troubles. For now! But Ferdy, smart and always near the surface, does realize that such good times don't last forever. He would have to face his troubles eventually.

But, for now, he was content to enjoy the moment. He was Ferdinand Fink, the accomplished actor—after all, look where he'd gotten so far— after only a few hours in Mexico—to the wedding of Gonzalez Gonzalez!

After a few rounds of drinks, Ferdy excused himself to go to the restroom. As he returns, he senses that a group of men are watching him. These are chilling men; three of them. They stop him.

"Who are you?"

"Who wants to know?"

"Look tough guy, if you don't want to be a puddle on the floor, just answer the question."

Hmm, maybe I'd better tone down and back off the big-screen macho-man bit.

"Just call me Ferdy. I'm an actor."

"You are *El Buitre Cantor*. Don't bullshit us!"

Wthout further explanation he is taken upstairs to Gonzalez Gonzalez after first taking a moment to let Lara-Bianca know that he would be back soon.

After a little in-depth questioning, Gonzalez is clear that Ferdy is not *El Buitre Cantor*.

"Hey, *Amigo*, you know how to handle *un pistola*?"

Ferdy knows that he has no choice but to accept where this is going. He is desperate for a new life, but he wants to actually *live* that new life.

"Look, Senor Gonzalez, I'm an actor, not a killer."

"Listen to me. You are *El Buitre Cantor*. You are The Singing Vulture! If I say you are *El Buitre Cantor*, you are *El Buitre Cantor*. Gonzalez pulls out a minature .45 and points it at Ferdy's feet.

"If you are to be *The Singing Vulture*, you must at least yodel." Yodel for me!

*   *   *

Gonzalez Gonzalez gives Ferdy his first assignment: to assassinate a rival crime lord. Ferdy is terrified, but he knows he must do it.

It happens, too, Ferdy learns later from Lara-Bianca, that Lara-Bianca is Gonzalez's only daughter!

El Buitre Cantor, *The Singing Vulture*, appropriately, and somewhat fatefully, begins to hum the tune of Bob Dylan's *Simple Twist of Fate!*

As days go by, it is no longer tolerable to the couple (Ferdinand and Lara-Bianca have fallen in love) that she continue to be in her father's house. Ferdy is able to stall Gonzalez on his plan that Ferdy kill Javier. Gonzalez has no idea Lara-Bianca and Ferdy have hit it off.

*   *   *

Ferdy and Lara-Bianca meet in secret, hidden from Gonzalez Gonzalez's watchful eyes. They knew that they must be careful, but they were determined to find a way to outsmart Gonzalez and escape.

"We need to come up with a plan," said Ferdy. "Gonzalez Gonzalez is a powerful man. He has many deadly resources at his disposal, but we have something that he doesn't have. We have each other!" [*Editor's note:* That's almost as trite as "Oh, the humanity," but I had to leave it there for its cuteness value—and, those were Bard's exact words. No editing added.]

Lara-Bianca nodded. "Together, we are smarter than he is," she said. "And we're more resourceful. We'll find a way to beat him."

"And we know that he will not harm his daughter. You, on the other hand, Ferdy, are in deep doo-doo," she laughed.

They talked for hours, brainstorming ideas to come up with a plan. They knew that they had to be careful and meticulous. If they made even one small mistake, Gonzalez Gonzalez would be onto them.

They came up with a plan that they thought would work. It was risky, but their only chance.

The next day, Ferdy went to Gonzalez Gonzalez and told him that he was ready to kill Javier Javiero. Gonzalez was pleased. He had been waiting many years to get Javiero.

"Good," he said. "Now go and do what you must do."

*   *   *

Ferdy went to talk to Javier Javiero, but not to kill him. Instead, he informed him of the death plan. Javier was hesitant at first to cooperate, but Ferdy convinced him to help.

"Javier, I need your help. I have a plan to defeat Gonzalez Gonzalez, but I can't do it without you."

"I'm listening."

"We have Lara-Bianca to help us.

"His daughter?"

"Yes. She's on our side."

"I'm not sure I trust her. She is, after all, Gonzalez's daughter!"

"I trust her. We are lovers. And besides, there is no choice. We need her help or I will have to kill you."

"Alright. I'll do it."

"Now, tell me more about this plan, Ferdy."

"We need to create a distraction. Something that will get Gonzalez's attention away from me."

"What kind of distraction?"

Ferdinand Fink, the actor, always thinking great theater, responds, "What if we stage a fake robbery?"

"We could rob one of Gonzalez's casinos, but we wouldn't actually take any money. We would just make a lot of noise and commotion. Gonzalez would be so focused on the robbery that he wouldn't pay attention to us. At this point, Lara-Bianca tells them about the ledger.

* * *

Ferdy Fink and Javier Javiero burst into Gonzalez Gonzalez's office, guns drawn. Gonzalez looks up from his desk, his eyes wide in surprise and sudden fear.

"What is this?"

"We're here for the ledger."

"Only if I'm dead first!" Gonzalez screams.

Gonzalez goes for the gun in his desk drawer, but Ferdy is faster. He fires a shot into Gonzalez's shoulder. Gonzalez screams in pain as he rolls to the floor. Too many empanadas!

Javiero grabs the ledger and runs out of the office. The Gonzalez Gonzalez swat team is waiting for them in the hallway.

A gunfight ensues. Even with much bobbing and weaving, Fink and Javiero are outnumbered and outgunned. They fight back bravely, but in vain.

Javier is shot in the leg, but manages to keep fighting. Ferdy takes out two of Gonzalez's men and fights on.

It looks like curtains for the good guys. But wait! Are these really good guys? At this moment they seem like simple bush league robbers. All we need are cops and we've got ourselves a good children's game going. Stay tuned, because. . . .

Just when it seems like all will be lost, Lara-Bianca bursts through the smoke-filled hallway, a gun firing away in each hand. She takes out the remaining two of Gonzalez's men. Growing up with a crime lord has advantages. But, one of her bullets has gone astray. Poor Ferdy! How ignominious. He is shot in the buttocks!

Ferdy and Javier both run—well, Ferdy sort-of runs. Hobble-hops would be more like it—to Lara-Bianca, as Javier collapses to the floor, bleeding badly from the leg wound.

"Are you okay?" Lara-Bianca asks Ferdy.

Ferdy nods. "I'm fine, so long as I don't sit down, thanks to you! Wait, I didn't mean it that way."

Lara-Bianca smiles broadly. "You're welcome."

Ferdy hobble-helps Lara-Bianca to heft Javier out of the casino. They make it to a waiting car and speed away. Ferdy is kneeling on the back seat. "Well! We need a back-window lookout, don't we?"

Gonzalez's men follow in pursuit, but the "hero car," powered by no-knock premium high-test gasoline, manages greater speed and escapes.

They drive to a safe house where Javier's wounds are tended to. Javier will be okay, but he must rest for a few weeks. Ferdy is okay too—and his rubber dough-nut will be very helpful.

They had the ledger. They were safe. But the fight wasn't over. Gonzalez would be back for them.

Ferdy, Javier, and Lara-Bianca could relax for a bit.

Ferdy and Lara-Bianca had each other. Javiero was aware, too, that when he *really* got away, he'd be safe too, AND!! this was the biggest safety factor of all, they had the truth on their side. They now could not be defeated.

They opened the ledger. It was filled with evidence of Gonzalez Gonzalez's criminal activities—drug trafficking, money laundering, and murder.

"This is it," Ferdy said. "This brings him down."

Checking in at the Puerto Something-or-other ho-tel, where Ferdy first started, and they were total un-knowns, the three of them spent the next few days going through the ledger, making copies of the most important documents. They contacted the police and provided them with the evidence.

The authorities launched a raid on Gonzalez Gon-zalez's operations and he was arrested. Charged with multiple felonies, and murders, he was sentenced to life in prison.

Ferdinand Fink, Javier Javiero, and Lara-Bianca Gonzalez had defeated Gonzalez Gonzalez. They had used the ledger to bring him to justice, and they had made the world a safer place.

As Gonzalez Gonzalez was perp-walked off that day, in handcuffs, Ferdy went up to him and said, "I told you, Gonzalez. I told you I was going to defeat you."

Gonzalez Gonzalez glared at Ferdy. "This isn't over. I'll get out of here, and when I do, I'll come for you."

Ferdy smiled. "I'll be waiting for you—with Lara-Bianca and your grandchildren," he said.

www.ingramcontent.com/pod-product-compliance
Lightning Source LLC
Chambersburg PA
CBHW021350060726
47591CB00006B/2248